GYM BATTLE GUIDEBOOK

BY SIMCHA WHITEHILL

Scholastic Inc.

CONTENTS

HELLO, TRAINER!

Do you love to battle with your Pokémon pals? Are you always thinking of your strategy? Are you up for a challenge? Well then, you are ready to begin your journey as a Pokémon Trainer!

There are so many cool Gyms and amazing Trainers to battle with all over the world. You might be wondering: Where do you go to find these matches? Who do you look for to challenge? What are the rules of the battle? What Pokémon will you face? Which one-of-a-kind badges can you collect? This guidebook will give you the inside scoop on all the details you need to know as you battle your way from Gym to Gym to the glory of a regional tournament—and battles against the Elite Four!

GYM BATTLES

Scattered across the globe are unique battle houses known as Gyms. Each Gym is managed by a talented local Pokémon Trainer. On your journey, your goal is to seek them out and ask them to battle. Some Gym Leaders will easily say yes, others might need some convincing, and a few might even give you another challenge first.

Once you do battle them, if you have a smart strategy and end up winning, the Gym Leader will reward you with a special Gym badge that you can only earn at their particular Gym. And if you want to enter the big regional Tournament, you must earn all the badges in that regional League.

If you do not win your match against a Gym Leader, don't give up! You can continue training hard with your Pokémon in the hope that you can prove you deserve a rematch. In other words: If at first you don't succeed, try, try again!

And you are off to a great start! This guidebook will give you the tools and knowledge you need to be your best in each battle.

KANTO REGION

Trainers who journey through Kanto with the
hope of earning Gym badges will participate
in the Indigo League. When a Trainer has
completed their mission and filled their badge
case with all eight badges, they will be granted
a spot at the regional Indigo Conference. This
important tournament is held on the Indigo
Plateau at the famous Indigo Stadium.

BROCK

PEWTER GYM

GYM LEADER: Brock

LOCATION: Pewter City

TYPE SPECIALTY: Rock-type

POKÉMON ON HAND: Steelix, Crobat, Geodude, Mudkip, Ludicolo, Forretress, Croagunk, Chansey, Sudowoodo, Marshtomp

BATTLE: 2-on-2

BADGE: Boulder Badge

FUN FACTS

▌▶ Brock's dream is to become the best Pokémon breeder. This Gym Leader is also an expert at caring for Pokémon and especially good at cooking for them. His skills extend to cooking for people, too, and he can whip up a gourmet meal even over a campfire.

▌▶ Brock is really a lover, not a fighter. He falls for every girl he meets.

▌▶ Brock is the oldest of ten siblings and has also been their guardian. He loves his brothers and sisters more than anything, and they love him right back.

▌▶ The Pewter Gym is built with big boulders— and the battlefield is also full of sizable stones.

▌▶ Brock will accept any challenge for the Boulder Badge. All a Trainer has to do is visit his Gym and ask.

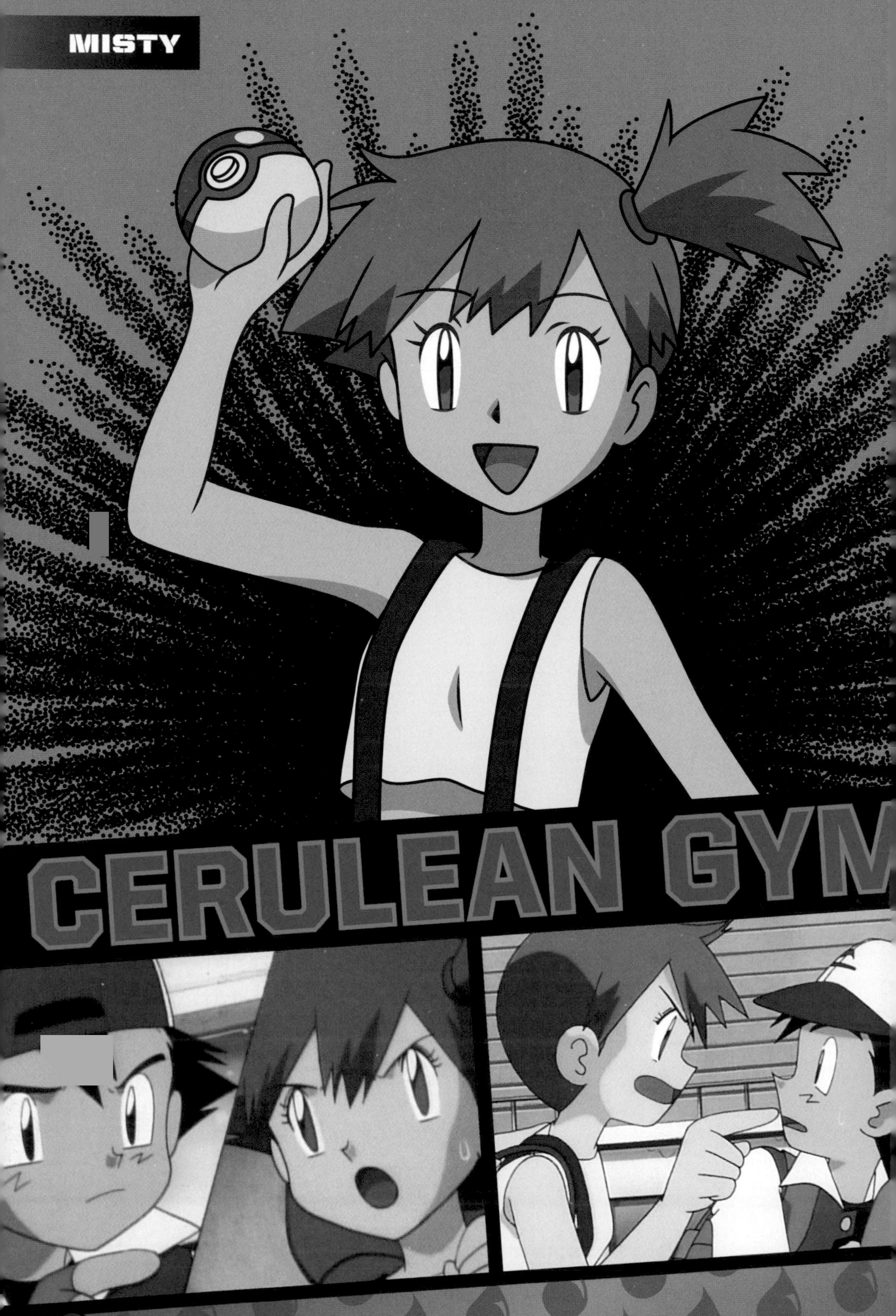

CERULEAN GYM

GYM LEADER: Misty

LOCATION: Cerulean City

TYPE SPECIALTY: Water-type

POKÉMON ON HAND: Starmie, Goldeen, Horsea, Psyduck, Politoed, Togetic, Corsola, Azurill, Luvdisc

BATTLE: 2-on-2

BADGE: Cascade Badge

FUN FACTS

▐▶ You can't miss the colorful Cerulean Gym! It has a pink-and-orange-striped dome roof with a giant Dewgong sitting in its wavy trim. Inside is a big pool, a high-diving board, and plenty of seats for all the fans who have come to see Misty's stunning siblings, better known as the Sensational Cerulean City Synchronized Swimming Sisters.

▐▶ Sisters Lily, Violet, Daisy, and Misty used to share the responsibilities and title of Gym Leader. Although her older sisters considered her the "runt," Misty was determined to learn all she could about Pokémon battles, and she traveled far and wide to study them. Her sisters were so focused on their water ballet that they hardly liked to battle and had been known to offer a Trainer the Cascade Badge without accepting a challenge. This was unacceptable to Misty, and she returned home to be the sole Cerulean Gym Leader full-time. Her sisters are now the ones traveling on a world tour.

▐▶ If Misty accepts your challenge, be prepared to battle while standing on a platform in her huge Gym pool.

▐▶ The Cascade Badge is a handmade work of art. Each one is crafted by Mr. Kinzo in Rafore Village.

GYM LEADER: Lt. Surge

LOCATION: Vermilion City

TYPE SPECIALTY: Electric-type

POKÉMON ON HAND: Raichu

BATTLE: 1-on-1

BADGE: Thunder Badge

FUN FACTS

▮▶ You'll know you're in the right place to battle Lt. Surge if you spot a building marked with bright yellow lightning bolts flashing across it.

▮▶ The only thing that packs a bigger zap than a bolt is Lt. Surge's harsh words. This trash-talking Gym Leader will hit challengers with his smack talk before they even step onto the battlefield. He doesn't bother with names and prefers to call each Trainer "baby."

▮▶ Lt. Surge doesn't hold back with his moves either. He's been known to send Trainers and Pokémon alike to rest at the Pokémon Center after a bout with him. But don't let this big bully scare you. If it's a Thunder Badge you're after, there is only one way to get it—you have to be bold enough to battle Lt. Surge!

GYM LEADER: Sabrina

LOCATION: Saffron City

TYPE SPECIALTY: Psychic-type

POKÉMON ON HAND: Kadabra

BATTLE: 1-on-1

BADGE: Marsh Badge

FUN FACTS

▌▌ Sabrina and her Pokémon partner, Kadabra, are of one mind. They are able to share thoughts without speaking! Kadabra isn't the only one with Psychic powers—the Gym Leader herself is a master of telekinesis, the mysterious art of using the mind to control objects and sometimes even people. At her Gym, Sabrina has many students studying telekinetic power in the hope of improving their skills with Psychic-type Pokémon.

▌▌ Sabrina has also been known to have an eerie partner with her—a spooky little girl that represents her as a child. Together, they have been known to turn challengers at the Gym into dolls! Consider yourself warned.

▌▌ Your best hope in a battle against Sabrina is choosing a Ghost-type, especially if it has a silly sense of humor.

CELADON GYM

GYM LEADER: Erika

LOCATION: Celadon City

TYPE SPECIALTY: Grass-type

POKÉMON ON HAND: Tangela, Weepinbell, Gloom

BATTLE: 3-on-3

BADGE: Rainbow Badge

FUN FACTS

⏩ In a town full of fabulous shops and department stores, one special perfume boutique stands out—because its manager is also the local Gym Leader, Erika!

⏩ If you're looking to challenge Erika, head to a structure that resembles the Flower Pokémon Vileplume. This big building holds a greenhouse full of plants, a Pokémon habitat, a perfume factory, and a battlefield. Likely, you'll be greeted by one of her helpful scent experts. When they introduce you to Erika, be sure to compliment her pretty perfumes before you ask for your battle challenge.

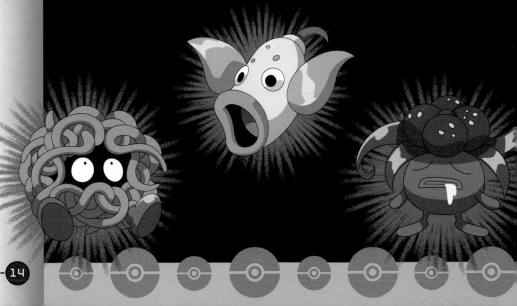

GYM LEADER: Koga

LOCATION: The forest by Fuchsia City

TYPE SPECIALTY: Poison-type

POKÉMON ON HAND: Venomoth, Golbat

BATTLE: 2-on-2

BADGE: Soul Badge

FUN FACTS

▷ No road leads to the Fuchsia Gym. It is buried deep in the woods and doubles as a secret ninja training camp.

▷ From afar, its emerald-green tile roof might blend in with the treetops, but up close there is no mistaking that this Gym is a mega mansion.

▷ Beware: This Gym is full of traps, secret doors, and even tilted floors!

▷ Look out: Koga's sister Aya might surprise you with throwing stars!

GYM LEADER: Blaine

LOCATION: Inside a volcano on Cinnabar Island

TYPE SPECIALTY: Fire-type

POKÉMON ON HAND: Ninetales, Rhydon, Magmar

BATTLE: 3-on-3

BADGE: Volcano Badge

FUN FACTS

▶ Much to Blaine's dismay, Cinnabar Island has become a popular destination for tourists who like to soak in its hot springs. So, the Gym Leader abandoned his Gym in town and is hiding out where you'd never expect to find him—a hotel! Blaine runs the Big Riddle Inn.

▶ You might not recognize Blaine, because he wears a disguise. And he's just as sly with his words: He speaks in riddles. If you want to challenge Blaine to a battle, you'll first have to play his word games.

▶ Here are three helpful hints:

  o His inn is marked by a clock tower.
  o To open the secret entrance to his hidden Gym, tap on the head of the Gyarados statue.
  o Be careful: The door handle is burning hot.

GYM LEADER: Giovanni

LOCATION: Viridian City

TYPE SPECIALTY: Ground-type

POKÉMON ON HAND: Persian, Golem, Kingler

BATTLE: 3-on-3

BADGE: Earth Badge

FUN FACTS

▌▶ Giovanni has another job aside from Gym Leader, which has made him infamous: He's a villain! Greedy Team Rocket calls him "Boss." He likes to poach Pokémon.

▌▶ He has a taste for the finer things in life: His peach-colored Gym is lined with white columns, and its entrance has a double staircase, a fountain, and golden doors.

▌▶ The Gym is guarded by two giant men in armor who grant entry to one Trainer at a time. If you make it past them, you'll find Giovanni perched on a balcony overlooking the battlefield with his preferred Pokémon part-ner, Persian. From his armchair, Giovanni chooses and commands Pokémon to battle challengers.

ORANGE ISLANDS

Trainers who journey across the ocean to the Orange Islands can seek Gym battles for unique badges that resemble seashells.

GYM LEADER: Cissy

LOCATION: Mikan Island

TYPE SPECIALTY: Water-type

POKÉMON ON HAND: Seadra, Blastoise

BATTLE: Cissy does not have traditional battles with Trainers at the Mikan Gym. Matches are decided by two challenges, in which Pokémon compete like athletes in tests of their strength, skill, and agility.

BADGE: Coral-Eye Badge

FUN FACTS

▶ Challengers can spot the orange Gym roof from afar—it peeks above the tree line.

▶ You might see Cissy's little brother before you arrive. He keeps watch and likes to set silly traps along the path to taunt Trainers. Don't be bothered by him: Keep your eye on the badge prize!

▶ Once Orange Crew member Cissy accepts your challenge, you'll get to see her cool Gym. Hidden under the floor is a huge pool, perfect for Water-type Pokémon. The wall opens up onto a beach, where you might have a Water Gun–firing contest to test your aim, or even a Wave Ride challenge, where you hop on your Pokémon partner's back for a speedy swim.

▶ Whatever the competition, you and your Pokémon partner should be prepared to show off your sporty side.

GYM LEADER: Danny

LOCATION: Navel Island

TYPE SPECIALTY: N/A

POKÉMON ON HAND: Nidoqueen, Scyther, Machoke, Electrode, Geodude

BATTLE: Danny does not have traditional battles with Trainers at the Navel Gym. Matches are decided by three tests, in which Pokémon and Trainers compete like athletes in competitions of strength, skill, and agility.

BADGE: Sea Ruby Badge

FUN FACTS

▶ In the center of Navel Island is a giant mountain that is so high that its peak is hidden by clouds and covered in snow. If you decide to challenge Orange Crew member Danny, you'll first have to rock-climb to the mountaintop to convince him to accept your request—even though there's a cable car running up to the peak.

▶ Danny loves outdoor adventures. As a Trainer seeking the Sea Ruby Badge, you'll get the chance to compete with him in a few of his other favorite sports, like sailing and sledding. You and your Pokémon partners just might find yourselves carving an ice sled for a steep downhill race.

▶ Challenges at the Navel Island Gym are fast and fun!

GYM LEADER: Rudy

LOCATION: Trovita Island

TYPE SPECIALTY: N/A

POKÉMON ON HAND: Electabuzz, Exeggutor, Starmie, Hitmonchan, Golem, Alakazam, Rhydon, Venomoth, Ninetales

BATTLE: Every Trainer must first pass a test of skills before Rudy accepts their challenge. For example, you could be asked to have your Pokémon fire at targets along the shore as you boat around the island. If successful, the Trainer will have the chance to choose three Pokémon of different types to participate in traditional battles. Rudy will then choose Pokémon with the same three types to face them. The Trainer must win two out of three battles to earn the Spike Shell Badge.

BADGE: Spike Shell Badge

FUN FACTS

▶ The entrance to the Trovita Gym is marked by a smile made of glass with a Poké Ball in the middle.

▶ Gym Leader Rudy is a true romantic and a fabulous dancer! At his practices, he likes to turn on some tunes and groove with his Pokémon and kid sister, Mahri.

▶ The battlefield itself is in the ocean on one of the giant rock spikes that surround the island. Spectators cheer from a hot air balloon, and the referee surveys the scene on a Pidgeot.

GYM LEADER: Luana

LOCATION: Kumquat Island

TYPE SPECIALTY: N/A

POKÉMON ON HAND: Alakazam, Marowak

BATTLE: A Double Battle: a battle between pairs of Pokémon.

BADGE: Jade Star Badge

FUN FACTS

▶ Kumquat Island is a popular vacation spot in the Orange Islands, and Luana doesn't just run the local Gym: She is also in charge of one of the fanciest hotels in the area.

▶ Many Trainers like to stay at Luana's Kumquat Hotel, and not just because they want to challenge Luana. There is a studio inside the hotel where Pokémon can take aerobics classes to help with their training.

▶ For those who are there to battle, the hotel boasts an amazing stadium with a referee who wears a suit and bow tie. Luana is an Orange Crew member who takes her battling seriously!

JOHTO REGION

To compete in the celebrated Silver Conference in Silver Town at the foot of Mt. Silver, a Trainer must earn all eight Johto League Gym Badges. More than two hundred Trainers enter in this impressive competition.

GYM LEADER: Falkner

LOCATION: Violet City

TYPE SPECIALTY: Flying-type

POKÉMON ON HAND: Pidgeot, Hoothoot, Dodrio

BATTLE: 3-on-3

BADGE: Zephyr Badge

FUN FACTS

▌▌ Gym Leader Falkner always dreamed of flying as a kid. Now, he wants to be known as the best Flying-type Trainer who ever lived! And he doesn't just leave the air to his Pokémon pals—he has mastered riding the wind himself by hang gliding. He also loves soaring through the sky with his pal Pidgeot.

▌▌ To challenge Falkner, head to the tall purple spiral tower in town. On the roof is a round, open-air battlefield where you will get the chance to take him on.

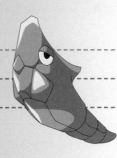

GYM LEADER: Bugsy

LOCATION: Azalea Town

TYPE SPECIALTY: Bug-type

POKÉMON ON HAND: Spinarak, Metapod, Scyther

BATTLE: 3-on-3

BADGE: Hive Badge

FUN FACTS

▷ As you may be able to guess from his name, Bugsy is obsessed with Bug-types. He lives by the motto "The Trainer who learns the rules of the Bug Pokémon learns to rule the Bug Pokémon." And he has dedicated his training and Gym to his beloved Bug-types.

▷ The Azalea Gym is a giant greenhouse with a glass dome. Inside, you'll find a forest filled with plants, trees, and Bug-type Pokémon. In the middle is a dirt battlefield where Bugsy promises all challengers who trek out to his Gym a chance to earn the Hive Badge.

GOLDENROD GYM

GYM LEADER: Whitney

LOCATION: Goldenrod City

TYPE SPECIALTY: N/A

POKÉMON ON HAND: Miltank, Nidorina, Clefairy

BATTLE: 3-on-3

BADGE: Plain Badge

FUN FACTS

- Even though Goldenrod City is big and crowded, you can't miss the Gym, with its red-domed roof. Perhaps it's so clearly marked because Gym Leader Whitney isn't great with directions and often loses her way in the busy city!
- Whitney really is most at home in the rolling hills near Goldenrod City, where her Uncle Milton runs a Miltank farm. It produces all kinds of Miltank products, from butter to cheese to flan, but it's best known for its nutritious cream that can help a Pokémon power up. Trainers on their way to challenge Whitney might want to stop there for a special drink!

ECRUTEAK GYM

GYM LEADER: Morty

LOCATION: Ecruteak City

TYPE SPECIALTY: Ghost-type

POKÉMON ON HAND: Gastly, Gengar, Haunter

BATTLE: 3-on-3. Only the challenger can substitute Pokémon.

BADGE: Fog Badge

FUN FACTS

▶ The Tin Tower is Ecruteak's most famous landmark. As the story goes, the Tin Tower was the only place the Legendary Pokémon Ho-Oh would make contact with humans. It was built to promote understanding between Pokémon and people. For generations, this sacred spot was guarded by Morty's ancestors. Ho-Oh would appear only to the guardians, and when it did, it was a good omen and a sign of peace. One day, greedy invaders came looking for Ho-Oh and set the tower on fire. Morty's ancestors left the burned building standing as a reminder of the horrible acts humans are capable of.

▶ Now, Gastly hide in the old tower and like to scare intruders.

▶ Morty's ancestors built a new Tin Tower that looks exactly like the old one, but Ho-Oh has not reappeared in three hundred years.

▶ The new Tin Tower acts as the local Gym and classroom. Morty sees teaching young people about Ghost-type Pokémon as part of his duty. If Morty accepts your challenge, expect his students to watch from the stands.

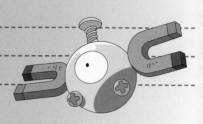

GYM LEADER: Jasmine

LOCATION: Olivine City

TYPE SPECIALTY: Steel-type

POKÉMON ON HAND: Steelix, Magnemite

BATTLE: 2-on-2

BADGE: Mineral Badge

FUN FACTS

▶ The entrance to Jasmine's Gym is marked with two tall columns topped with Poké Ball statues and big yellow letters.

▶ Another place in town that truly has Jasmine's heart is the Shining Lighthouse. Her grandfather, Myron, tends to it, and ships coming into the port depend on it. The lighthouse is lit by an amazing Ampharos named Sparkle. Thanks to this powerful Electric-type Pokémon, no electricity is needed to create the strong beam of light.

▶ When the lights come on at the battlefield at Jasmine's Gym, you'll want to double-check that you are battling the Gym Leader herself. Jasmine has an apprentice named Janina who is young, friendly, and anxious to prove her skills. If you end up facing a girl and her Onix, be aware that you are not in an official battle for the Gym badge.

GYM LEADER: Chuck

LOCATION: Cianwood City

TYPE SPECIALTY: Fighting-type

POKÉMON ON HAND: Machoke, Poliwrath, Machop, Mankey, Hitmontop

BATTLE: 2-on-2

BADGE: Storm Badge

FUN FACTS

▐▌ Chuck is a macho guy who has been known to battle even his Pokémon partners. He trains hard and he expects the same discipline from his challengers. In fact, if Chuck meets you in town, he might make you march all the way to the Gym!

▐▌ If Chuck does not escort you personally, you'll be able to spot the Gym by its bright blue tile roof.

▐▌ Many Trainers come to study with Chuck, and they all call him Master. Although he seems tough, Chuck has a soft spot for Fighting-type Pokémon, his pupils, and even his challengers. When you're at his Gym, Chuck will likely invite you to a meal with his crew—so arrive hungry for battle and also for lunch!

GYM LEADER: Pryce

LOCATION: Mahogany Town

TYPE SPECIALTY: Ice-type

POKÉMON ON HAND: Piloswine, Dewgong

BATTLE: 2-on-2. Only the challenger can substitute Pokémon.

BADGE: Glacier Badge

FUN FACTS

▐▶ Ice-type expert Pryce can be as cold as frozen water. If he doesn't think a challenger is worthy, he will reject their request for a Gym battle.

▐▶ Behind the stone walls of the gated Gym, it's truly a winter wonderland. The Mahogany Gym isn't just a haven for Trainers; it's also a chilly Pokémon habitat, complete with a lake. The battlefield itself is solid ice, with a pool in the middle and icy rocks scattered across it.

▐▶ While you're there, say hi to Sheila, the friendly Triple A judge for the Johto League. Thanks to her personality, she is the warmest thing at the Mahogany Gym!

GYM LEADER: Clair

LOCATION: Blackthorn City

TYPE SPECIALTY: Dragon-type

POKÉMON ON HAND: Kingdra, Gyarados, Dragonair

BATTLE: 3-on-3. Only the challenger can substitute Pokémon.

BADGE: Rising Badge

FUN FACTS

▶ Clair has always felt that she is responsible for protecting Pokémon, and she trained with the noble Lance of the Pokémon G-Men. As Gym Leader, she has also taken it as her responsibility to guard the nearby sacred Pokémon habitat and temple: the Dragon's Holy Land and Dragon Shrine.

▶ With the help of her friend Kaburagi, Clair cares for the precious Dragon Fang, which belonged to the first-ever Blackthorn Gym Leader.

▶ Clair has a special place in her heart for Dragon-types and a respect for history. But she will not hold back in battle, and neither will her Pokémon! If she accepts your challenge, be ready for a battlefield with a pool in the center.

HOENN REGION

The Hoenn League Championship is held in Ever Grande City. This extremely large tournament begins with a whopping six hundred competitors, all of whom have earned eight Gym badges in Hoenn.

GYM LEADER: Roxanne

LOCATION: Rustboro City

TYPE SPECIALTY: Rock-type

POKÉMON ON HAND: Nosepass, Geodude

BATTLE: 2-on-2. Only the challenger can substitute Pokémon.

BADGE: Stone Badge

FUN FACTS

▶ Roxanne splits her time between the Rustboro Gym and the Pokémon Trainer's School. If you challenge her, she will likely ask to record your match so she can use it for one of her lessons.

▶ Roxanne loves being a teacher and has her students intern at the Gym to get hands-on experience.

▶ Her incredible battlefield was made especially for Rock-type Pokémon, with stones and boulders all around. Even the outside of her Gym looks like a rock formation, and it would probably be hard to spot if it were in the mountains! Luckily, the Rustboro Gym stands out amid the other buildings in bustling Rustboro City.

PETALBURG GYM

GYM LEADER: Norman

LOCATION: Petalburg City

TYPE SPECIALTY: Normal-type

POKÉMON ON HAND: Slaking, Slakoth, Vigoroth

BATTLE: 3-on-3. Only the challenger can substitute Pokémon.

BADGE: Balance Badge

FUN FACTS

▮▷ Norman is something of a local celebrity. The people of Petalburg love him so much that they are even obsessed with his family, and they treat them as if they're famous. Norman can't blame his fans—he adores his wife, Caroline, and children, May and Max, too!

▮▷ May is a budding Pokémon Coordinator who competes in Pokémon Contests.

▮▷ When you arrive at the Petalburg Gym, you might be recognized! Max, Norman's son, will greet you by name if you're a challenger who has competed in a League Championship. Max loves to study battles, and he might highlight your losses, but don't let him fool you into thinking he's the Gym Leader.

▮▷ Norman is a fierce Gym Leader to face in battle. He isn't focused on wins or losses; he just enjoys the fun of battling—which is a hard concept for his competitive son, Max, to understand.

GYM LEADER: Brawley

LOCATION: Dewford Town

TYPE SPECIALTY: Fighting-type

POKÉMON ON HAND: Machop, Makuhita, Hariyama

BATTLE: 2-on-2. Only the challenger can substitute Pokémon.

BADGE: Knuckle Badge

FUN FACTS

▶ The entrance to Dewford Gym is beyond a golden arch with an emblem of Fighting-types Machop and Machoke, under a sign that says, "Fight the Big Wave!" This big Gym sits on a cliff overlooking the ocean.

▶ Brawley has a secret practice island just offshore. It can be reached only by a path that presents itself at low tide.

▶ This Gym Leader is also a surfer extraordinaire! He likes to be close to the beach so he can catch the waves when they're, as he would say, "gnarly." And if the waves are gnarly, your battle for the Knuckle Badge will have to wait: Brawley won't miss the chance to surf! He believes it's an important part of training his Pokémon. He uses surfing to help them build strength in their legs and to teach them balance. In fact, no matter where you live, Brawley thinks nature is the best guide for training.

GYM LEADER: Wattson

LOCATION: Mauville City

TYPE SPECIALTY: Electric-type

POKÉMON ON HAND: Magnemite, Voltorb, Magneton

BATTLE: 3-on-3

BADGE: Dynamo Badge

FUN FACTS

▶ Battling for the Dynamo Badge is a wild enough ride, but fun-loving Wattson likes to laugh and wants to amuse his challengers, too, so he turned the entrance to his Gym into a roller coaster!

▶ Wattson also has been known to playfully turn up the power and speed of the ride, despite his assistant Watt's pleas not to. Get ready, because the minute you step into Wattson's Gym, you'll find yourself in a cart winding up, down, and all around!

▶ The cart will pass the hallway and go through a water feature, and finally stop in front of a giant, roaring Raikou. But don't try to battle it—that Raikou is just a robot! Save your energy for Wattson and his Electric-type Pokémon.

LAVARIDGE GYM

GYM LEADER: Flannery

LOCATION: Lavaridge Town

TYPE SPECIALTY: Fire-type

POKÉMON ON HAND: Slugma, Magcargo, Torkoal

BATTLE: 3-on-3. Only the challenger can substitute Pokémon.

BADGE: Heat Badge

FUN FACTS

- Lavaridge Town is famous for its hot sand baths, hot springs—and even hot spring hot cross buns!

- Flannery's Gym might be a little disorganized, but she is certainly focused on bringing the heat in battle. She is sure to accept your challenge and invite you to her outdoor battlefield, which has a dirt floor.

- Flannery is the granddaughter of the famed Lavaridge Gym Leader Old Man Moore. He was passionate about poetry, and he decided to leave the Gym to Flannery so he could travel and work on his writing. But he only made it three days on his journey before he came back to help around his beloved home Gym. Now he acts as the judge for the badge matches, and Flannery is an enthusiastic new Gym Leader.

GYM LEADER: Winona

LOCATION: Fortree City

TYPE SPECIALTY: Flying-type

POKÉMON ON HAND: Altaria, Pelipper, Swellow

BATTLE: 3-on-3. Only the challenger can substitute Pokémon.

BADGE: Feather Badge

FUN FACTS

▶ If you fly into Fortree City, you might be able to spot the Fortree Gym battlefield because it sits atop the roof, open to the sky. But if you arrive on foot, you'll have to hike up the stairs at the front of the building to reach this beautiful battlefield with a view.

▶ Winona loves the open air, and both she and her Pokémon love to take to the sky. If you challenge the Flying-type expert, prepare to keep your head in the clouds during the match.

▶ When you arrive at the Gym, check in with her assistant Zachary. Winona will accept your challenge even if she is at the town's annual Feather Carnival, which celebrates the sky. To Winona and other locals, the sky is a truly sacred place.

▶ Before you try to make your first move in a match, wait for Winona. She always prays to the great blue world above before beginning a battle challenge.

GYM LEADERS: Tate and Liza

LOCATION: Mossdeep City

TYPE SPECIALTY: Psychic-type

POKÉMON ON HAND: Lunatone, Solrock

BATTLE: Double Battle, no substitutions. Tate and Liza each choose one Pokémon and the challenger will choose two. All four Pokémon will battle in pairs until one team is knocked out.

BADGE: Mind Badge

FUN FACTS

▌▶ A Gym battle with twins Tate and Liza feels truly out of this world! The battlefield, in the shiny dome of the Mossdeep Gym, has a floor full of craters and a night sky full of planets above it. As a challenger, you'll find your opponents floating, too! The twin Gym Leaders have an awesome aerial way of battling—in three dimensions, the way it would feel in outer space.

▌▶ You can expect Liza to choose Lunatone and Tate to choose Solrock for your match—both Pokémon who supposedly came from space.

▌▶ The twins love space because Mossdeep City is home to a famous Space Center, which launches shuttle missions, the Ho-Oh Three space probes, and the *Sunflora* weather satellite. In fact, Tate and Liza's father is the director of the Space Center and a top astronaut!

▌▶ Even though they are twins, Liza loves to tease Tate for being her "little brother," because he was born second.

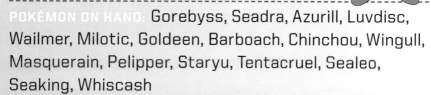

GYM LEADER: Juan

LOCATION: Sootopolis Island

TYPE SPECIALTY: Water-type

POKÉMON ON HAND: Gorebyss, Seadra, Azurill, Luvdisc, Wailmer, Milotic, Goldeen, Barboach, Chinchou, Wingull, Masquerain, Pelipper, Staryu, Tentacruel, Sealeo, Seaking, Whiscash

BATTLE: Challenger and Gym Leader select five Pokémon each. The first round is a Double Battle. The second round is a 3-on-3 battle.

BADGE: Rain Badge

FUN FACTS

▶ Juan does everything with grace and elegance, and puts on incredible performances featuring his well-trained Water-type Pokémon. They are so synchronized that when light hits their combined Water attacks, a rainbow spreads across the island.

▶ Before Juan became the Sootopolis City Gym Leader, he was a decorated Pokémon Coordinator. He even participated in the Grand Festival, and won a Ribbon Cup.

▶ At Juan's magnificent mansion and Gym, you're welcomed by Sebastian, Juan's butler and referee. The first round of battle is on a platform overlooking a pool, and then you'll switch sides with Juan as the battlefield is changed out for a lake with a grassy shore.

SINNOH REGION

To reach the peak tournament of the Sinnoh League, Trainers need to take the ferry to Lily of the Valley Island. There, they can enter the competition if they have earned eight Gym badges in the Sinnoh Region.

GYM LEADER: Roark

LOCATION: Oreburgh City

TYPE SPECIALTY: Rock-type

POKÉMON ON HAND: Rampardos, Geodude, Onix

BATTLE: 3-on-3. Only the challenger can substitute Pokémon.

BADGE: Coal Badge

FUN FACTS

◗ Roark calls his Gym, a stone structure in the mountainside, the "Temple for Rock Pokémon."

◗ You're not likely to find Roark hanging around his Gym, though, because he's also Chief of Ancient Pokémon Excavation Operations in the Oreburgh Mines. A man named Ian greets Trainers and cares for the Pokémon at the Gym. But Roark is always ready to accept battle challenges!

◗ The local mines are rich in coal ore, treasure, and—most important to Roark—Fossils. He loves the thrill of excavating an ancient Pokémon! He sends his Fossil finds straight to the local museum and research lab, where a special Fossil restoration machine can bring back to life the ancient Pokémon preserved in the rock. Then, researchers can observe their abilities and learn about Pokémon development.

GYM LEADER: Gardenia

LOCATION: Eterna City

TYPE SPECIALTY: Grass-type

POKÉMON ON HAND: Cherubi, Turtwig, Roserade, Bellossom, Vileplume, Victreebel

BATTLE: 3-on-3. Only the challenger can substitute Pokémon.

BADGE: Forest Badge

FUN FACTS

▶ Gardenia can't get enough of her favorite type of Pokémon! She likes to stroll through nearby Eterna Forest in the hope of catching more Grass-type Pokémon pals. And if a Grass-type already has a Trainer, she will try to make a trade.

▶ She is also willing to help travelers with good intentions find the amazing Combee Wall and precious Enchanted Honey in her treasured Eterna Forest. She likes to keep a low profile in the forest, though, and is not likely to admit that she is the Gym Leader.

▶ To find her Gym, look for an open-air stadium covered in vines and filled with trees and other plants. It has the ideal conditions for Grass-type Pokémon, especially Cherubi, who uses sunlight to supercharge its speed with its Chlorophyll Ability.

GYM LEADER: Maylene

LOCATION: Veilstone City

TYPE SPECIALTY: Fighting-type

POKÉMON ON HAND: Lucario, Meditite, Machoke

BATTLE: 3-on-3. Only the challenger can substitute Pokémon.

BADGE: Cobble Badge

FUN FACTS

▶ Maylene is a famous, well-respected Trainer, but a very new Gym Leader.

▶ Strong Maylene has even been known to spar with her Pokémon pal, Lucario, for training—with Lucario trying to train her!

▶ After a particularly hard loss to a nasty Trainer who called her "the weakest leader" he ever fought, Maylene lost her confidence—but luckily, not her friends. Lucario and the black belt fighters who study at the Veilstone Gym stood behind her and didn't let her give up her new leadership role. Challengers kept arriving, and Maylene eventually regained confidence through the joy she finds in battling.

GYM LEADER: Crasher Wake

LOCATION: Pastoria City

TYPE SPECIALTY: Water-type

POKÉMON ON HAND: Floatzel, Quagsire, Gyarados

BATTLE: 3-on-3. Only the challenger can substitute Pokémon.

BADGE: Fen Badge

FUN FACTS

▶ Wake is a giant Gym Leader with a big heart. He loves to see cooperation among Trainers and Pokémon, and he often compliments his challengers during battle.

▶ He's also a judge of the annual Pastoria Croagunk Festival. Pastoria City is located by the Pastoria Great Marsh, and the whole town prizes the marsh's popular inhabitant, Poison- and Fighting-type Pokémon Croagunk. In fact, every household in town raises a Croagunk. Once a year, Wake helps crown the new Croagunk Festival Diamond and Pearl Champion.

▶ Wake is an expert in Water-type Pokémon. The battlefield in his Gym is a long pool with many floating islands from which to attack.

GYM LEADER: Fantina

LOCATION: Hearthome City

TYPE SPECIALTY: Ghost-type

POKÉMON ON HAND: Drifblim, Gengar, Mismagius

BATTLE: 3-on-3. Only the challenger can substitute Pokémon.

BADGE: Relic Badge

FUN FACTS

▶ If you want to battle Fantina, you might just have to take a number. The Gym Leader is a free spirit who likes to travel to become even stronger. After all, she wants to give her challengers the best battle possible!

▶ Fantina is hardworking and passionate. She has two goals. One, she loves Contest battling and has been training to become a Top Coordinator. Two, Fantina dreams of creating a new style of battling that combines the beauty of competition with the fierceness of the battlefield. With her dedication to her craft, it's no wonder Trainers are lining up for the chance to battle her!

▶ Her favorite kind of match is a rematch. Fantina appreciates the effort of challengers who step up their training to improve their skills so they can return to her Gym.

GYM LEADER: Byron

LOCATION: Canalave City

TYPE SPECIALTY: Steel-type

POKÉMON ON HAND: Bronzor, Steelix, Bastiodon

BATTLE: 3-on-3. Only the challenger can substitute Pokémon.

BADGE: Mine Badge

FUN FACTS

▷ In addition to being the Canalave Gym Leader, Byron loves to dig up Fossils at Iron Island nearby.

▷ Byron is the father of Oreburgh Gym Leader Roark, who also loves digging Fossils—and they are huge rivals. This father and son have been known to battle on and off the field: Byron has dedicated his life to Fossils and won't be outdone by his son.

▷ Deep down, Byron truly loves and treasures his son. His prized possession is the first Fossil Roark gave him: a Sunkern leaf. In fact, the only reason Byron left Oreburgh City for Canalave City was so he could give his son a Gym of his own to run. But his gesture was misunderstood: Roark thought that his dad ran away.

GYM LEADER: Candice

LOCATION: Snowpoint City

TYPE SPECIALTY: Ice-type

POKÉMON ON HAND: Sneasel, Medicham, Snover, Abomasnow

BATTLE: 4-on-4. Only the challenger can substitute Pokémon.

BADGE: Icicle Badge

FUN FACTS

▶ Gym Leader Candice is also well-known as Ms. Senior, a teacher at the Pokémon Trainers' School. Candice herself was a student there years ago. Most classes are geared for students up to age ten: The school's mission is to teach these future Trainers the basics of handling Pokémon. However, Ms. Senior teaches a special class for older Trainers.

▶ She likes to shout out, "Kiai!" to encourage others to go for it—in everything from a battle to a pop quiz!

▶ Be prepared to go for it yourself if Candice accepts your battle challenge on her icy field in the wintry wonderland that is Snowpoint City.

GYM LEADER: Volkner

LOCATION: Sunyshore City

TYPE SPECIALTY: Electric-type

POKÉMON ON HAND: Electivire, Jolteon, Luxray

BATTLE: 3-on-3. Only the challenger can substitute Pokémon.

BADGE: Beacon Badge

FUN FACTS

❯❯ Volkner has a reputation for being an electrifying Trainer. However, when he first became a Gym Leader, he doubted himself and lost his zest for battles. He would refuse any battle challenge and would simply hand out badges to any Trainer who asked for one. Luckily, he regained his spark with the help of Ash and his dear old friend, Elite Four member Flint.

❯❯ In addition to being an Electric-type Pokémon expert, Volkner also knows a lot about electricity. Because of him, Sunyshore City runs on solar power! Solar panels all over town are charged by the sun, and this energy is sent to the local power plant, Sunyshore Tower. Volkner built the tower, which is also a rocket that can use solar energy to take flight! Volkner truly is a multi-talented guy. If you get the chance to challenge him, be sure to bring your spark!

UNOVA REGION

The biggest championship in the Unova League has been known to register 128 challengers, each of whom have earned eight Gym badges in the region. To enter the intense competition, head to the stadium in Vertress City.

CILAN

STRIATON GYM

GYM LEADERS: Cilan, Chili, and Cress

LOCATION: Striaton City

TYPE SPECIALTY: Grass-type (Cilan);
Fire-type (Chili); Water-type (Cress)

POKÉMON ON HAND: Pansear, Panpour, Pansage, Dwebble

BATTLE: 1-on-1 with the challenger's choice of one of the
Gym Leaders

BADGE: Trio Badge

FUN FACTS

▐▌ Cilan, Chili, and Cress are triplets who share the title of Gym Leader at the Striaton Gym.

▐▌ Good news for those who don't like to battle on an empty stomach: The entrance to the Gym is a fancy and popular restaurant. Challengers, be sure to mind your manners when you order your food, or the three restaurant-owning brothers might not accept your battle request.

▐▌ Cilan is not only a restaurateur and Gym Leader, he is also an aspiring Pokémon Connoisseur—someone who judges the compatibility of Trainers and their Pokémon pals to help them form closer bonds.

GYM LEADER: Lenora

LOCATION: Nacrene City

TYPE SPECIALTY: Normal-type

POKÉMON ON HAND: Watchog, Lillipup, Herdier

BATTLE: 2-on-2 with substitutions allowed for both the Gym Leader and challenger.

BADGE: Basic Badge

FUN FACTS

▶ The Nacrene Gym is also a very important museum, where the knowledgeable Gym Leader Lenora and her husband, Hawes, are curators. The halls are filled with incredible artifacts, including suits of armor, a meteorite, and the largest skeletal model of Dragonite.

▶ A special wing of the museum is reserved for researchers and challengers: the library. Hidden in the shelves is the secret route to the Gym. Lenora will test challengers by suggesting they read a specific book, but many Trainers will want to pick another book they're more interested in. Listen to Lenora! That book she shares with you is the only key that opens the door to the Nacrene Gym.

CASTELIA GYM

GYM LEADER: Burgh

LOCATION: Castelia City

TYPE SPECIALTY: Bug-type

POKÉMON ON HAND: Dwebble, Whirlipede, Leavanny

BATTLE: 3-on-3

BADGE: Insect Badge

FUN FACTS

▶ Burgh considers himself an artistic Trainer because he is a fashion designer, an artist, and a Gym Leader. He is devoted to his craft and to Bug-types.

▶ Like every great artist, Burgh once found himself in a slump. So he decided to live in Pinwheel Forest among and like the wild Pokémon. Surrounding himself with nature renewed his spirit and creativity!

▶ If you challenge Burgh, expect a battle with passion and flair!

GYM LEADER: Elesa

LOCATION: Nimbasa City

TYPE SPECIALTY: Electric-type

POKÉMON ON HAND: Tynamo, Zebstrika, Emolga

BATTLE: 3-on-3. Only the challenger can substitute Pokémon.

BADGE: Bolt Badge

FUN FACTS

▶ The Nimbasa Gym arena is full of bright neon lights, and the stands are packed with fans.

▶ Beautiful supermodel and Gym Leader Elesa can draw a crowd! She likes to stage fashion shows and walk the runway, but she shines even brighter in battle, thanks to her Electric-type Pokémon pals. Those who challenge Elesa for the Bolt Badge get an electrifying show!

GYM LEADER: Clay

LOCATION: Driftveil City

TYPE SPECIALTY: Ground-type

POKÉMON ON HAND: Krokorok, Palpitoad, Excadrill

BATTLE: 3-on-3. Only the challenger can substitute Pokémon.

BADGE: Quake Badge

FUN FACTS

▌▌ Gym Leader Clay is a fast-talking businessman and a successful miner. He first started digging with a pickax with his pal Excadrill long ago. That's how he earned the title "King of the Mines." Even his Gym battlefield is in a mine!

▌▌ Good luck getting Clay to accept your challenge. He is a busy guy, known to push off a battle request from a Trainer many times. Be persistent, and prepare to jump through a hoop or two and be called a "whippersnapper." Just don't give up easily if it's a Quake Badge you're after.

GYM LEADER: Skyla

LOCATION: Mistralton City

TYPE SPECIALTY: Flying-type

POKÉMON ON HAND: Swoobat, Unfezant, Swanna

BATTLE: 3-on-3. Only the challenger can substitute Pokémon.

BADGE: Jet Badge

FUN FACTS

⫸ If you see a building that looks like an airplane hangar with a sign that reads, "Mistralton Cargo Service," you have arrived at the local Gym! Gym Leader Skyla is obsessed with flying planes.

⫸ Skyla has earned a reputation for being so awesome at battles that she has been overwhelmed by challengers. She might have fifteen Trainers lined up to battle her—and that was just in one group of morning appointments!

⫸ Skyla tried to save time by inventing an imaginary form of battling called "Air Battles." Luckily, she returned to real battles after many Trainers were frustrated and her grandfather (the previous Mistralton Gym Leader) was upset.

GYM LEADER: Brycen

LOCATION: Icirrus City

TYPE SPECIALTY: Ice-type

POKÉMON ON HAND: Vanillish, Cryogonal, Beartic

BATTLE: 3-on-3. Only the challenger can substitute Pokémon.

BADGE: Freeze Badge

FUN FACTS

- If you're a film buff, you might recognize Brycen from martial arts movies, like the blockbuster *Enter the Beartic*. Although he made a string of successful action movies, Brycen stepped out of the limelight after an accident on set. He felt he needed more training with his best buddy, Beartic, to prevent another mishap.

- Bryce spends his days at the nearby mountain sanctuary protecting the wild Pokémon from greedy Pokémon hunters.

- Bryce's Icirrus Gym Ice Castle is built into a mountainside and has big blue doors that slide open when challengers arrive. As the name suggests, it's freezing inside the Gym! Be sure to bring a warm coat.

GYM LEADER: Roxie

LOCATION: Virbank City

TYPE SPECIALTY: Poison-type

POKÉMON ON HAND: Koffing, Scolipede, Garbodor

BATTLE: 6-on-3 battle. The challenger gets to choose twice as many Pokémon as the Gym Leader has.

BADGE: Toxic Badge

FUN FACTS

▌▌ Roxie the Gym Leader is also the band leader of a popular punk rock trio called Koffing and the Toxics. Backed by her bandmates and wearing (and occasionally playing!) a bass guitar, Roxie takes on challengers during her concerts. At her battles, the music is loud and the crowd is even louder!

▌▌ To challenge Roxie, look for an unremarkable dark blue door. Go down the stairs and you'll find her at the underground rock club and Gym.

KALOS REGION

Head to Lumiose City Stadium to enter the biggest battle in the region, the Kalos League Tournament! This can be a particularly exciting competition because of the likelihood of battles with Mega Evolving Pokémon.

GYM LEADER: Viola

LOCATION: Santalune City

TYPE SPECIALTY: Bug-type

POKÉMON ON HAND: Surskit, Vivillon

BATTLE: 2-on-2. Only the challenger can substitute Pokémon.

BADGE: Bug Badge

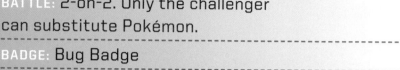

FUN FACTS

▌▶ Viola is a photographer who focuses on capturing pictures of her favorite Bug-type Pokémon. Inside the Santalune Gym is a gallery featuring her artwork. She has also been known to snag shots for her older sister, an acclaimed journalist named Alexa.

▌▶ To challenge Viola, head to her green Gym building in town. Inside, the battlefield looks like a greenhouse. It is lined with trees and other plants and gets plenty of light thanks to the glass roof.

GYM LEADER: Grant

LOCATION: Cyllage City

TYPE SPECIALTY: Rock-type

POKÉMON ON HAND: Onix, Tyrunt

BATTLE: The Gym Leader has the use of only two Pokémon; the challenger has the use of all the Pokémon they currently have on hand.

BADGE: Cliff Badge

FUN FACTS

▶ An elevator leads to the Gym battlefield, but Grant suggests that challengers take a more difficult route. He invites Trainers to scale the tall rock-climbing wall because he sees it as a way to share his great love of rocks with them.

▶ Grant also sees the hard climb as a chance for challengers to focus their minds on the task in front of them and reach a state of inner peace that prepares them for battle.

▶ If you decide not to climb, Grant swears it doesn't mean that he won't accept your challenge. Which risk will you take, Trainer?

SHALOUR GYM

GYM LEADER: Korrina

LOCATION: Shalour City

TYPE SPECIALTY: Fighting-type

POKÉMON ON HAND: Lucario, Mienfoo, Machoke

BATTLE: 3-on-3. Only the challenger can substitute Pokémon.

BADGE: Rumble Badge

FUN FACTS

- The Shalour Gym is located inside the Tower of Mastery.

- Korrina comes from a long line of Trainers who have Lucario as their Pokémon partner.

- One of Korrina's ancestors discovered Mega Evolution by helping their Lucario Mega Evolve. Mega Evolution is a process by which a Pokémon powers up during battle. It is a temporary and extremely strong state that requires three critical elements:
  - o a strong bond between Trainer and Pokémon
  - o a Key Stone
  - o a species-specific Mega Stone.

- Korrina and Lucario together won 100 battle challenges in a row before they even began to look for the Lucarionite Mega Stone. Korrina wanted to ensure that her friendship with Lucario was unbreakable before attempting Mega Evolution.

- Korrina always races around Kalos on roller skates! She knows she might hit a few bumps in the road as she speeds through Kalos, so she always wears a helmet and pads for safety.

- There's only one way to get to the Mega Evolution Island where the Tower of Mastery stands. When the time is right and the tide changes, a path appears through the sea. Only then can a challenger proceed to the Tower of Mastery and find the Shalour Gym inside.

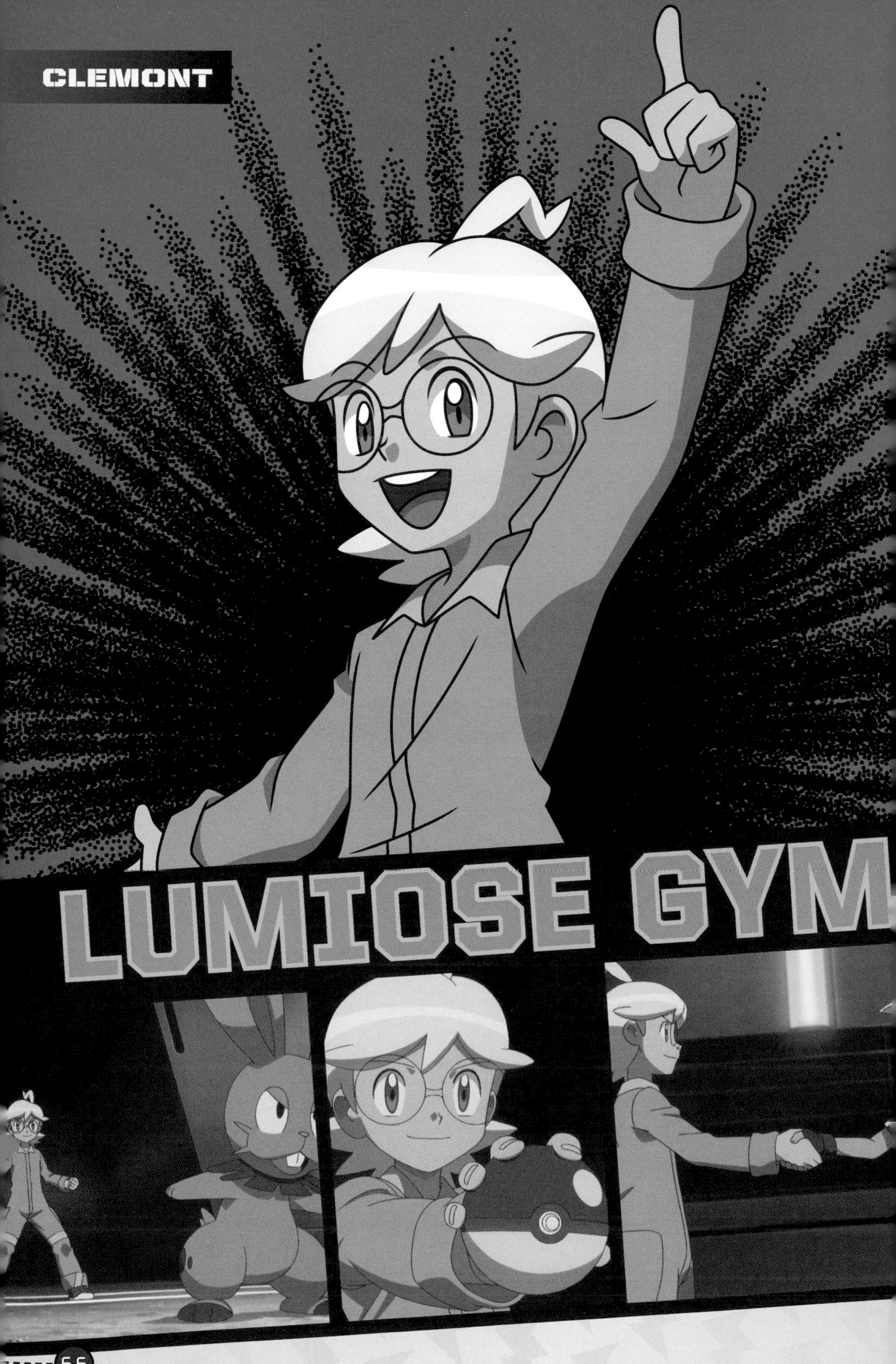
LUMIOSE GYM

GYM LEADER: Clemont

LOCATION: Lumiose City

TYPE SPECIALTY: Electric-type

POKÉMON ON HAND: Luxray, Bunnelby, Chespin, Dedenne, Magnemite, Heliolisk

BATTLE: 3-on-3. Only the challenger can substitute Pokémon.

BADGE: Voltage Badge

FUN FACTS

▶ Clemont's Gym is located in a Lumiose City landmark: the Prism Tower.

▶ Clemont is an inventor who has created many machines with varying results. A few of his most successful gadgets are:

  o the Aipom Arm he uses to grab things (like his sister)

  o the Clemontic Shower, which can recharge Electric-type Pokémon

  o Clembot, a robot that greets challengers at his Gym

▶ Be warned: If you meet Clembot, it will immediately ask if you have earned at least four Gym badges in Kalos. If you answer no, Clembot will zap you with an electric jolt and then eject you from the Gym. It is one strict robot! It also referees Clemont's Gym battles.

▶ Clemont's little sister, Bonnie, is constantly by his side, and they love spending time together. Clemont even caught her Pokémon pal Dedenne!

▶ Clemont's father, Meyer, is also a superhero known as the Blaziken Mask. Whenever there is trouble in Lumiose City, Meyer and his Mega Evolving Blaziken will swoop in and save the day!

GYM LEADER: Ramos

LOCATION: Coumarine City

TYPE SPECIALTY: Grass-type

POKÉMON ON HAND: Jumpluff, Weepinbell, Gogoat

BATTLE: 3-on-3. Only the challenger can substitute Pokémon.

BADGE: Plant Badge

FUN FACTS

▌▶ Ramos owns a private ranch habitat for Grass-type Pokémon, but his Gym is in a giant, old tree. To get to the treetop battlefield, climb the steps that wrap around the trunk.

▌▶ When you arrive, Gym Leader Ramos might ask you to help tend his garden and pull weeds. Ramos loves how gardening helps challengers calm their minds and see what's important right in front of their eyes.

GYM LEADER: Valerie

LOCATION: Laverre City

TYPE SPECIALTY: Fairy-type

POKÉMON ON HAND: Sylveon, Spritzee, Mr. Mime, Mawile

BATTLE: 2-on-2. Only the challenger can substitute Pokémon.

BADGE: Fairy Badge

FUN FACTS

▶ Valerie is a famous fashion designer who does everything with flair. Inside her Gym, she even has a store where she sells her fabulous outfits.

▶ Valerie regularly throws thrilling runway shows for her new collections. Her designs feature fabrics with patterns inspired by Pokémon, like Azumarill, Chingling, and Florges, and the clothes are all meant for battle. To demonstrate, at the end of her show she has been known to call up a Trainer to challenge, and turns the runway into a battlefield.

▶ If you happen to arrive on a day when there isn't a runway show, Valerie will still make quite a colorful entrance at the battlefield inside the Gym. Prepare to be dazzled by design!

GYM LEADER: Olympia

LOCATION: Anistar City

TYPE SPECIALTY: Psychic-type

POKÉMON ON HAND: Meowstic

BATTLE: Double Battle. No substitutions.

BADGE: Psychic Badge

FUN FACTS

▶ Mystical Lady Olympia has the power to predict the future, and she is not shy about sharing her visions. She has many apprentices who are in awe of her insight. She often uses her gift to protect Kalos' treasured landmarks, Pokémon, and inhabitants from evil.

▶ On the battlefield, she is nearly unbeatable because of her unique grasp of the past, present, and future. Olympia's battlefield might even remind challengers of the inner workings of a clock, since it sits atop golden gears.

▶ To find her, head to a shiny silver dome with three slanted gold arches stretching across it—the amazing Anistar Gym!

SNOWBELLE GYM

GYM LEADER: Wulfric

LOCATION: Snowbelle City

TYPE SPECIALTY: Ice-type

POKÉMON ON HAND: Abomasnow, Avalugg, Bergmite

BATTLE: 3-on-3. Only the challenger can substitute Pokémon.

BADGE: Iceberg Badge

FUN FACTS

▶ Snowbelle City is covered in a blanket of snow, and to find the Gym you'll have to trek up a mountainside.

▶ Inside the Gym, challengers get a warm welcome from Bergmite and a warning that the temperature of the battle-field will be frosty. Icicles hang from the ceiling, the floor is slippery ice, and Wulfric's Pokémon Abomasnow's Ability can even make it hail inside.

▶ While challengers might want a parka, Wulfric will be comfort-able sitting on his ice throne. No matter how low the temperature goes, a battle for the Iceberg Badge will get any Trainer fired up!

CHAMPION LEAGUE

ELITE FOUR

Being in the Champion League is incredibly prestigious, and the path to get there is unbelievably difficult. First, a Trainer must win eight Gym badges in their region to qualify for the local League Tournament. Next, that Trainer must win first place at that League Tournament. (For example, if a Trainer is from Hoenn, they must be the victor at the Hoenn League Championship in Ever Grande City.) Only then can that Trainer enter what is called the Champion League. In the Champion League, the Trainer must battle all of the regional Elite Four members—the top Trainers from the region. If the Trainer can beat the Elite Four, they will get the chance to officially battle their Master of the Champion League.

Becoming a member of the Elite Four is no small feat! The Elite Four in each region are admired and appreciated by all. Once they achieve greatness, they follow different paths. Read on to see how some of these champions have chosen to use their talent and their titles.

BRUNO

Indigo League Elite Four member Bruno is known for his speed in battle. Now he has a secret training spot somewhere on Mt. Hideaway. But don't bother trying to find him if you aren't willing to do everything he asks of his trainees. He would argue that there is no secret to training Pokémon, but he has his training methods and they require hard work. He has been known to make those who ask for his help perform difficult tasks. He might have you hauling buckets of water to improve your strength and balance, splitting wood to build a firm grip, and carrying stones uphill as a lesson in controlling your inner nature. He might also ask a Trainer to peel off the bark from a twig, but that will just be to make chopsticks to eat his delicious Bruno stew.

Bruno moved to Mt. Hideaway to catch a giant Onix. He also has Fighting-type Hitmonchan on hand. This Elite Four member believes that a strong Pokémon helps you become a strong Trainer.

Surprisingly enough, tough guy Bruno isn't quick to fight. Rather than attacking, he prefers to try to talk to a Pokémon first to be sure they're feeling okay. As Bruno has said, first and foremost, "Humans and Pokémon must live and work and share this world together and they must care for each other."

AGATHA

Don't underestimate Agatha because she's from an older generation. She might carry a walking stick, but she can also ride a bicycle, and there is no slowing her down in battle! She thinks fast and has years of experience on the battlefield. That combination has made Agatha one of the most impressive opponents you can ever face in battle. And she loves nothing more than a good challenge. You might be able to find her subbing as Gym Leader at the Viridian Gym with her Pokémon Gengar and Golbat. If you do get the chance to ask her for a match, she will likely say yes. Just be sure to bring your A game!

DRAKE

Hoenn Elite Four member Drake doesn't just battle Pokémon. He also battles the wildest waves as a ship's captain. He likes to invite people onto his big boat and share a cup of hot milk with peppermint, and then he might even be up for a match on the deck. If you get the chance to battle this legend, don't be fooled if he just stands there. He isn't giving up—he knows timing is everything. Drake doesn't have his Pokémon Shelgon, Altaria, and Salamence fire attacks willy-nilly. Instead, he waits for exactly the right moment to strike.

It's clear that Drake is confident. But he'll be the first to tell you that with experience came the wisdom to back up his skills. When he first began to feel like an impressive Trainer, he says, "I started believing I was unbeatable, going from battle to battle just to prove it. What had started as confidence had become overconfidence, and this was robbing me of my concentration in battle." Now, Drake frees his mind of all those other thoughts so that his ego doesn't get in the way of his ability to be present in a battle.

Young Trainers would be wise to listen to Drake's suggestions. He offers this advice: "Keep battling stronger opponents, but without arrogance or fear of defeat."

LUCIAN

The Psychic-type expert of the Sinnoh Elite Four is awesome to watch on television battling it out with his Pokémon Bronzong and Girafarig. If you're lucky enough to run into Lucian, he is likely to accept a request from another Trainer, but he is even more likely to agree to a battle with an eager Pokémon! Lucian is fascinated by Pokémon psychology and by what goes on in their hearts and minds. He believes in letting Pokémon express their emotions in battle as a way to gain strength.

After a Pokémon experiences a defeat, Lucian believes only that Pokémon can truly pick itself up and find the desire to go on battling. That battle spirit and desire to try new things and grow must come from within it. Even Lucian, with all of his success, believes he is still learning from each match—including the ones he wins.

To Lucian, the key is to find each Pokémon's special battle rhythm. The way he sees it, "A Trainer's task is to discover that unique style and help their Pokémon develop it!"

SINNOH

AARON

Fans line up for Aaron's autograph! He is famous for being one of Sinnoh's Elite Four. He's been on the cover of *Pokéchic* magazine and has performed shows with his Pokémon pals Drapion, Vespiquen, and Skorupi to stadiums full of adoring audiences.

Though he has a popular public persona, he prefers to live in a cabin he built himself. It sits in the middle of the woods, next to a lake, and is the perfect location for his beloved Bug-types.

As a young Trainer, Aaron was not naturally good at battling, which made him very insecure. He even called himself a "crybaby." When he was just beginning, he was so ashamed of his losses that he took out his anger on the one closest to him—his Pokémon partner Wurmple. He hurt Wurmple's feelings so much that it ran away. After that, Aaron was so heartbroken he put all his energy into training and understanding Bug-types. Aaron even learned their language: he possesses the extremely unique ability to understand what Bug-types are saying.

Later, while fighting Team Rocket, Aaron was reunited with his old pal Wurmple at the very same tall tree where they first met—though Wurmple had evolved into a beautiful Beautifly! While they'd been apart, both Beautifly and Aaron had spent their time training to be the best they could be. And after meeting again, it didn't take long for them each to realize that the best they could be is together!

FLINT

Flint is a Fire-type expert with a spark. He's ready to accept a battle challenge from any Trainer!

Growing up on the rough streets of Sunyshore City, Flint and his Pokémon pal Chimchar had to fight their way through every day. Flint still battles with Infernape by his side! He also remains friends with Volkner, the Sunyshore Gym Leader. Back when they were kids, Flint and Volkner challenged each other every day to see who was the best Trainer in town. But they were truly equals, and one day, they teamed up against a Pokémon Poacher spotted in the area. From then on, Flint and Volkner were good friends. Eventually, Volkner became a Gym Leader and Flint focused on improving his skills as a Trainer. But Flint still has Volkner's back, and when Volkner refused to battle Ash, or anyone, for a badge, it was Flint who was able to get his friend back on the battlefield.

Flint has honed his skills over years of practice. He's so confident, he always lets his opponent strike first! He believes it helps him learn and sharpen his skills. Flint is never intimidated by a challenger. As he says, "Only a person who truly believes they can win can win!"

BERTHA

Ground-type expert Bertha is herself very grounded: She's sensible and gives great advice to Trainers. In fact, her number-one piece of advice to Trainers is to "observe." So keep your eyes on your Pokémon, your opponent, and your surroundings if you want to battle like Bertha.

Bertha studies every situation before acting, but she's not slow, especially when she's behind the wheel. She drives fast and makes her moves even faster. Along with her powerful Pokémon pals Gliscor, Golem, and Hippowdon, Bertha assesses the scene quickly, and then strikes!

So, if you're looking for guidance, you might want to find Bertha, who likes to mentor young Trainers. However, she'd prefer if you didn't mention she is a member of the Elite Four. She likes to keep her status a secret and let her battle style speak for itself.

CAITLIN

She may seem as delicate as a flower petal, but Caitlin is a mighty Trainer who just happens to have a gentle personality. The Psychic-type expert is so cool and calm on the battlefield, you could forget she's in the middle of making her move. But make no mistake—this member of the Unova Elite Four is a fierce foe.

Nothing about Caitlin is casual. Her tone in conversation is very polite and formal, and she embodies the word "elegance." Even her arrival onto the battlefield is carefully crafted: She often makes a spectacular entrance where she does something like float down to the ground on a giant rosebud. And the way Caitlin makes a move is just as important to her as the move itself. In her words, "My ultimate goal is to win all battles with elegance and grace."

MALVA

Malva is a multitalented member of the Kalos Elite Four, but she hasn't always used her skills and smarts for good—and didn't always know how to choose her friends wisely.

When Malva was an on-air reporter at the Kalos League Tournament, Team Rocket was her camera crew. (They're not a trio anyone should trust with their image!) Malva was also a former member of the vicious Team Flare. She followed their power-hungry leader, Lysandre, as he attacked Lumiose City and attempted to take over the world. But just in the nick of time, she had a change of heart. Ash inspired her to use her battle strength for a righteous reason—to help kids like him and his friends stop Lysandre from destroying the world as they knew it. They succeeded, and she also helped bring the rest of her Team Flare comrades to justice. And it was all because some passionate kids helped her believe that the future could be better!

Malva has a heroic heart, and a deep bond with her loyal Pokémon pal, a Mega-Evolving Houndoom. She's proven herself worthy of the Kalos Elite Four and continues her commitment to fight for the good of the world.

HALA

When Ash first met Hala, he was best known as the wise kahuna of Melemele Island. But since the Alola Pokémon League was established, he also became a member of the Alola Elite Four.

While Hala's main focus is still protecting and caring for his beloved home island Melemele, he also makes Z-Rings by hand. The Island Guardian and Legendary Pokémon Tapu Koko gave one of Hala's special Z-Rings to Ash.

Kahuna Hala is also happy to give out Island Challenges to Trainers who ask. Those who pass their initial challenge then face an even greater one—the Grand Trial. In a Grand Trial with Kahuna Hala, a Trainer could battle Hala's Pokémon, Fighting-types Hariyama and Crabominable, and if successful, the Trainer could earn the Z-Crystal FightiniumZ.

But before the battle, spiritual Hala asks Trainers to visit the Ruins of Conflict with him for a grounding ceremony. And he's always available to lend an ear or offer advice as a friend. As he says, "When we're searching for life's answers, we should always look to our friends for help."

ACEROLA

Alola Elite Four member Acerola is a focused Trainer and an even more dedicated reader. You can often find her in the stacks of the library on Ula'Ula Island. She loves reading to the kids that come visit her, and she's as brave as the heroes she reads about. Acerola is a Ghost-type Trainer who is comfortable with anything eerie. Nothing freaks her out: not a haunted house, not a Pokémon thief—not even Mimikyu! In fact, one of her best friends is one such creepy Mimikyu she nicknamed Mimikins. (You can tell it's her Pokémon pal by the pretty pink flower on its ear.)

Acerola's other Pokémon on hand is the Puppet Pokémon, Shuppet. It appears all Ghost-types flock to her and her big heart, including the mysterious and misunderstood. When she encountered the mischievous spirit and thief Greedy Rapooh, she

took the time to understand that this thief was just a lonely Gengar looking for company.

Indeed, she's a friend to all. When Ash visited Ula'Ula, Acerola led him through the Haina Desert wasteland to meet Tapu Bulu, and even the prickly Island Kahuna Nanu considers her a good pal: Nanu gifted her Mimikium Z, the special Z-Crystal that will work with her buddy Mimikins.

ALOLA

OLIVIA

Alola Elite Four member Kahuna Olivia cares for the people and Pokémon of Akala Island along with Island Guardian and Legendary Pokémon Tapu Lele. Rock-type expert Olivia is likely to be found with her Pokémon Lycanroc and Probopass and a bunch of other friends— she makes friends everywhere she goes!

Olivia adds fun to everything she does, from hosting the Wela Fire Festival to managing an arts and crafts shop to leading a field trip for the Pokémon School, to holding a Grand Trial. She's known for her delicious Akala Curry, and has even sent Trainers on a search for the secret ingredients for it as part of her Island Challenge.

Good-natured Olivia is interested in hearing the stories of all the Trainers and Pokémon she meets, and enjoys encouraging and teaching young Trainers. If a Trainer decides to challenge her, she will be their cheerleader—even though they are her opponent! And if that challenger should win their Grand Trial, Olivia will gladly give them the Z-Crystal Rockium Z.

KAHILI

Before becoming a member of the Elite Four, Kahili was already a star athlete in Alola's most popular sport: Pokémon Golf. It's a unique game played on well-manicured fields that are also wild Pokémon habitats. (You might even spot a rare Pokémon like Shaymin on the greens in Alola!) In the game, Trainers hit a small ball with a club and then their Pokémon partner uses its skills to help direct the ball to a hole in the ground.

No one loves Pokémon Golf like Kahili, though she's occasionally felt burned out by the pressure of being a star, and losing hurts her confidence. Luckily, Kahili plays with a Pokémon partner who truly cares for her: a Toucannon she calls Touckey. Touckey doesn't even need to ask which golf club Kahili wants to use—it just hands her the right one. Then, Touckey can add some oomph to Kahili's shots and sink a hole in one with a Tail Wind gust!

Touckey can tell when Kahili is feeling overwhelmed, and it will act like her bodyguard to protect her. Or if she needs to be cheered up, Touckey will find a way to get her back in the swing of things. Kahili knows she can succeed with Touckey by her side.

MASTERS

Every League has talented Trainers working hard and caring for their Pokémon, but only one Trainer can be called the Champion League Master! Even more prestigious than being a member of the Elite Four is the honor of being called Champion.

How do they become the number-one Trainer in their region? It takes a lot of confidence, hard work, and partnership with their Pokémon. First, a Trainer must become a member of a League's Elite Four. Then, they must challenge the current Champion Master of that League—a battle so important and interesting, it's broadcast on television.

If the challenger can defeat the Champion in battle, then they've proven they are the strongest Trainer, and are named the Champion League Master. It's an amazing achievement!

LANCE

Lance is known as an undisputed Champion of the Indigo Elite Four, which is a united title for the regions Kanto and Johto. But perhaps his most important battles are undercover as a member of the Pokémon G-Men, a group of dedicated detectives who travel the world to stop anyone mistreating Pokémon. He regularly goes undercover and has infiltrated the most evil organizations, including Team Rocket, Team Magma, and Team Aqua. Danger could be Lance's middle name, because he does not shy away from any situation, no matter how intense. He is a man on a mission to protect and serve Pokémon!

LANCE'S POKÉMON

DRAGONITE

DRAGON POKÉMON
Height: 7'03"
Weight: 463.0 lbs.
Type: Dragon-Flying
Fun Fact: Dragonite is also one of Lance's favorite ways to travel. Flying on his buddy's back, he can swoop in and save the day!

GYARADOS

ATROCIOUS POKÉMON
Height: 21'04"
Weight: 518.1 lbs.
Type: Water-Flying
Fun Fact: After Team Rocket forced Gyarados to evolve, Lance rescued it from their evil clutches.

STEVEN STONE

STEVEN STONE'S POKÉMON

Steven Stone is known to spend his days researching and searching for rare, precious rocks linked to Pokémon Evolution and species-specific Mega Stones. But Steven doesn't hoard these to get rich—he's actually already wealthy. (His father, Stanwick, is the president of the biggest company in Hoenn, the Devon Corporation.) Instead, Steven is all about studying the powerful rocks and stones for the good of everyone. He's even been known to give out some to worthy Trainers.

And when there is trouble afoot, Steven Stone will step in and stand up to the evildoers, whether it's Team Rocket, Team Flare, or both! After he helped foil Lysandre's plan to destroy the world with the Giant Rock, he continued to study its remains to be sure it would do no more harm.

ARON

IRON ARMOR POKÉMON
Height: 1'04"
Weight: 132.3 lbs.
Type: Steel-Rock
Fun Fact: Aron helped Steven on his mission to find a Fire Stone in Granite Cave.

AGGRON

IRON ARMOR POKÉMON
Height: 6'11"
Weight: 793.7 lbs.
Type: Steel-Rock
Fun Fact: Aggron blasted Team Rocket right out of Granite Cave with Hyper Beam.

METAGROSS

IRON LEG POKÉMON
Height: 5'03"
Weight: 1212.5 lbs.
Type: Steel-Psychic
Fun Fact: Because of their deep bond of friendship, Steven Stone's Metagross can Mega Evolve.

CYNTHIA

Champion Cynthia hails from Celestic Town. There, her grandmother Carolina runs the important Historical Research Center. Cynthia herself is very interested in Legendary Pokémon and studies their stories. She dreams of knowing the Legendary Pokémon Dialga and Palkia, and of discovering the origin of all Pokémon.

When Cynthia was younger, she just wanted to be a powerful Trainer and win all of her battles. But as she met more and more Pokémon, she realized how unique each and every one truly was, and she changed her goal: She wanted to get to know all the Pokémon she was lucky enough to meet in her travels. Along the way, she became an unstoppable Pokémon Trainer! She rose up to be Champion Master—a title that hasn't been easy to hold on to. Sinnoh Elite Four members Lucian, Aaron, and Flint have all challenged her, but Cynthia has triumphed!

CYNTHIA'S POKÉMON

GARCHOMP

MACH POKÉMON
Height: 6'03"
Weight: 209.4 lbs.
Type: Dragon-Ground
Fun Fact: Garchomp is known for its especially effective Giga Impact blast.

ALDER

Alder, the Champion Master of Unova, is a local legend, but he's also very approachable. Young Trainers can ask him anything! He is full of advice that he's happy to share—but outside of Pokémon, he doesn't take much seriously. He might accept your battle challenge, but he also might not stay awake for it, and whatever happens, he definitely won't remember your name correctly—just ask "Ashton," aka Ash!

But Alder's arrogance can be an asset, and he has an unmatched patience for Pokémon. When a giant Gigalith was on a rampage through town, and no one knew how to stop it, Alder stepped up. Instead of attacking it, he put himself on the line to find what was behind Gigalith's anger. As it turned out, Gigalith had stepped on a nail and was in terrible pain. Alder cared for the Pokémon and ended everyone's suffering. It's no wonder so many young Trainers look up to him!

Alder tries to use his platform as Champion Master of Unova to work toward people and Pokémon living in perfect harmony. As he says, "Of course I want to become strong—but I also want people who see me battle to grow closer to Pokémon, just as I want Pokémon to grow closer to people! And that's the kind of battling I live for."

ALDER'S POKÉMON

BOUFFALANT

BASH BUFFALO POKÉMON
Height: 5'03"
Weight: 208.6 lbs.
Type: Normal
Fun Fact: If you get the chance to battle Bouffalant, beware of its hard-to-dodge Head Charge!

DIANTHA

Diantha is a multitalented superstar! Not only is she a Champion Master, she's also the lead actor in famous films such as *My Sweet, Sweet Lady*. And she performs live Exhibition Battles in stadiums packed with adoring fans.

As a result, her schedule is very tight—which her publicist will be happy to tell you as she shoos you away. It's hard for anyone, even an old friend like the well-respected Professor Sycamore, to get the chance to see her! But Diantha doesn't mind being so busy. She says, "I do it out of love. So it's really not work at all."

Diantha also finds time for yet another passion—dessert! Wherever this diva travels, she is sure to stop by all the famous sweet shops to satisfy her sweet tooth.

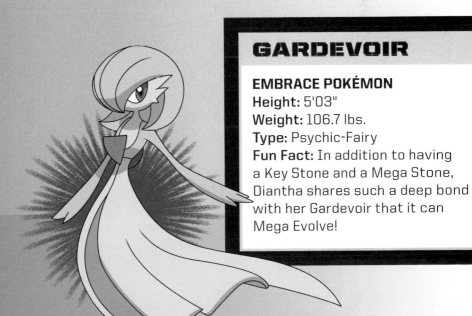

GARDEVOIR

EMBRACE POKÉMON
Height: 5'03"
Weight: 106.7 lbs.
Type: Psychic-Fairy
Fun Fact: In addition to having a Key Stone and a Mega Stone, Diantha shares such a deep bond with her Gardevoir that it can Mega Evolve!

DIANTHA'S POKÉMON

ASH KETCHUM

You may have already heard of the first Champion Master of Alola . . . He's an adventurous Trainer named Ash, from Pallet Town in the Kanto Region! Since the day he turned ten, he's been traveling the world with his trusty Pokémon Pikachu to become the best Trainer he can be. Together, they've worked hard, played hard, and made friends with many Pokémon and people along the way.

In Alola, Ash notably found a friend in the Legendary Pokémon Tapu Koko, the Guardian of Melemele Island. Tapu Koko watched over and battled Ash, and ultimately gave Ash his first Z-Ring and Z-Crystal. This let Ash use his first Z-Move with Pikachu, a powerful 10,000,000 Volt Thunderbolt!

Ash knew even the best Trainers have a lot to learn, and he was very curious about Z-Moves, so, he enrolled himself in the famous local Pokémon School. His teacher was Professor Kukui (also known as the famous Trainer and television star the Masked Royal), whose hope was to help start a battle League in Alola, just like other regions had. Together, Ash and the professor were both able to see their dreams become reality. After an open call for Trainers to compete, the Alola League was born at the Manalo Conference, and Ash and his Pokémon won its highest honor—Champion Master of Alola!

PIKACHU

MOUSE POKÉMON
Height: 1'04"
Weight: 13.2 lbs.
Type: Electric
Fun Fact: Ash and Pikachu won the Exhibition Match of the Alola Pokémon League against Professor Kukui and Tapu Koko with their shockingly powerful Z-Move 10,000,000 Volt Thunderbolt!

MELMETAL

HEX NUT POKÉMON
Height: 8'02"
Weight: 1763.7 lbs.
Type: Steel
Fun Fact: Ash's Melmetal evolved from Meltan just before the Alola Pokémon League Finals!

LYCANROC

WOLF POKÉMON
Height: 2'07"
Weight: 55.1 lbs.
Type: Rock
Fun Fact: Ash's Lycanroc is a very rare green-eyed Dusk Form.

GOOD LUCK, TRAINER!

Being a Pokémon Trainer is the adventure of a lifetime. By now, you're an expert, ready to pursue your own journey with your Pokémon! Everywhere you turn, there will be new experiences, new Gyms, new battles, new personalities, new challenges, and best of all, new Pokémon.

So if you're the kind of Trainer who is always ready for more fun, then there's only one thing left to do: *GOTTA CATCH 'EM ALL!*™